RUNAWAY FRED

ROSEMARY DEBNAM
CLAUDIO MUÑOZ

BLue BaNaNas

For Connie, who shared my
childhood doggy adventures,
and for Isabelle, Chloe
and Alexander
R.D.

RUNAWAY FRED

ROSEMARY DEBNAM
CLAUDIO MUÑOZ

HEINEMANN

Titles in the series:

Big Dog and Little Dog Visit the Moon
The Nut Map
Dilly and the Goody-Goody
Tom's Hats
Juggling with Jeremy
Baby Bear Comes Home
The Magnificent Mummies
Mouse Flute
Delilah Digs for Treasure
Owl in the House
Runaway Fred
Keeping Secrets

First published in Great Britain 1997
by Heinemann and Mammoth, imprints of Reed International Books Ltd
Michelin House, 81 Fulham Road, London SW3 6RB
and Auckland, Melbourne, Singapore and Toronto
Text copyright © Rosemary Debnam 1997
Illustrations copyright © Claudio Muñoz 1997
The Author and Illustrator have asserted their moral rights
Paperback ISBN 0 7497 2681 4
Hardback ISBN 0 434 97481 1
1 3 5 7 9 10 8 6 4 2
A CIP catalogue record for this title
is available from the British Library
Produced by Mandarin Offset Ltd
Printed and bound in China

My sister always wanted a dog.

She asked Mum and Dad for one,

but they said, 'No!'

So my sister saved her money
and bought a puppy. She brought it
home after school one day.

Mum was mad.

'Take that dog right back,' she said.

'Oh, please can't we keep him,' I said.

'He's sweet.'

Just look at those paw marks!

'What's he called?'

I asked my sister.

'Prince,' she said.

Mum laughed.

The puppy was round and fat,

like a fluffy pudding with legs.

9

'Dogs are not easy to look after,'
Mum said.

'You'll have to walk him every day,'
said Dad. 'And feed him and keep
him clean.'

'We will.

We will,'

we said.

The puppy stayed.

We named him Fred.

Mum bought Fred a collar
and lead. Dad bought him a disc
with his name and address on it.

12

We bought him a bowl for food and one for water. We made Fred a bed from an old washing up bowl. We put a cushion in it to make it soft and warm and cosy.

Come on, Fred, this is for you.

We found an old ball for Fred to play

with, but he liked socks better!

Sometimes Fred spilt his water,

but we mopped it up.

Sometimes he made puddles on the floor.

We mopped those up too!

Once Fred got Dad's slipper. He chewed a hole in it. We patched it with some sticky tape and hoped Dad wouldn't notice. But he did!

Mum had a coffee morning and Fred found some hats and coats to play with.

Fred wasn't really bad – except when

he kept running away.

Whenever anyone opened the front door,

Fred dived through it, 'Whooooosh!'

At first my sister and I chased after him.

We called his name.

We took a biscuit for him.

But we couldn't catch him.

A neighbour brought him back.

'Fred was found barking at

Mrs Tilly's chickens,' she said.

'Mrs Tilly was very upset.'

Goodness me!

The next time there was a knock at

the door, a policewoman stood there.

'Here's Fred,' she said.

Bad boy,
Fred!

'Do you know where we found him?'

'No,' we said.

'He jumped on a bus and ran upstairs. He rode all the way to town. We had to bring him back in a police van. Make sure you keep him on a lead in future.'

Fred loved riding on the bus.

People told us they had even seen him

waiting in the queue at the bus stop.

24

We tried hard to keep Fred in.

We put his lead on every time we took

him for a walk, but somehow he always

managed to escape.

Fred came to school one day.

He bounded into the classroom when

our teacher was reading us a story.

He wagged his tail and licked the teacher.

26

Everyone laughed and shouted.

Mum came with Fred's lead. She had

chased him all the way from home.

She was cross.

Then one day when Fred got out

he came home by himself.

He wasn't running.

He ran across the road and...

He was limping badly.

Some friends told us he had been

run over by a car.

Dad asked the vet to look at him.

Fred had to have his leg put in a splint.

He didn't like the splint.

He pulled the bandage off with his

sharp teeth and chewed it up.

We had to call the vet again.

Steady on, old chap.

29

When Fred's leg had healed,
he stayed in all the time.
'Good dog,' we said.
We cuddled him and gave
him extra biscuits.

Look, Mum.
He's being good.

One more,
Freddy.

Then, one day when Mum was
paying the milkman,
'Whooooooosh!'
Fred ran away again.

Come back here,
you little terror!

We were sad.

'I hope the police don't get him,' I said.

'He'll be OK,' my sister said.

'Let's go and look for him.'

We looked at the bus stop.

We looked in the park.

We looked in the school playground.

We looked in Mrs Tilly's garden.

But we didn't find him.

Finally, Fred came home by himself.

He had a teddy bear in his mouth.

'Bad dog,' we said, as we hugged him.

'Where did you get that bear?

That bear belongs to someone.'

I put the bear on my bedroom shelf.

We thought about how we could find

the owner of the bear.

We wrote a card and pinned it

to the tree next to the garden gate.

FOUND

yellow bear
with red coat
and black boots

No one came for the bear.

Then Fred got out again.

That afternoon he came back

with another bear!

I put it on the shelf next to the bear

with the red coat and the black boots.

How did Fred get those bears,

we wondered.

One day, coming home from school,

we saw Fred in the park.

He was running along next to a baby

buggy. The baby was holding a bear!

That night when Fred came home

we told him, 'No! No more bears.

That's stealing!'

But Fred didn't understand and soon

we had a whole shelf full of bears.

And a dinosaur.

And a rabbit.

And an elephant!

We put another card on
the tree by the gate.
Mum told her friends.

We told our teacher.
She put a card on the
school noticeboard.

42

Some people came to claim the bears.

And the rabbit...

Hoppity

We've found Dina at last!

And the dinosaur...

44

And the elephant.

45

But no one wanted the bear in the
red coat and the black boots.
So we left it on the
bedroom shelf.

Fred's grown up now. He doesn't run away any more. Now everyone loves Fred. Mum buys him special doggie treats. Dad doesn't even mind when Fred sits in his favourite chair.

And we still keep the bear to remind
us of when Fred was a bad
runaway puppy.